MUSKET AND MOBCAP

A Story of a Young American Patriot

By S.T. Davis

MUSKET AND MOBCAP

A Story of a Young American Patriot

By S.T. Davis

Text & Illustrations Copyright © 2011 by S. T. Davis

ISBN-10: 1-886166-29-3
ISBN-13: 978-1-886166-29-5

Pyramid Publishing Inc.
PO Box 8339
Utica, New York 13505
www.pyramidpublishingservices.com

CONTENTS

ACKNOWLEDGEMENTS

I would like to thank my critique group, Wish Upon A Word (Lianna Mahoney, Irene Uttendorfsky, and Joann White), for all their encouragement, support and helpful critiques. In addition I thank my daughter, Sandra, for encouraging me to print this book and V.T. Dacquino for his help with research and for writing his book, *Sybil Ludington, The Call to Arms*. Finally, I would like to acknowledge my sister, Nancy T. Barnes and K.L. Going, for their assistance and helpful suggestions.

PREFACE

Sybil Ludington (1761–1839), her family, and Enoch Crosby (1750–1835) were real people who lived during the American Revolution. Many of the events in this book really took place. Sybil lived with her father and mother and seven brothers and sisters: Rebecca (1763), Mary (1765), Archibald (1767), Henry (1769), Derick (1771), Tertullus (1773), and Abigail (1776). Sybil rode forty miles to muster her father's militia troops and Enoch spied for the Committee on Safety, both helping to thwart the efforts of the Loyalists to fight on the side of the British during the American Revolution. The rest is imagination.

STAR
Chapter One
1776, 25 August

I watched my horse take a long drink. The sun's rays made little rainbows through the beaded sweat on Star's neck. My own sweat stung my eyes and trickled down the center of my back. The drone of insects filled the hot summer air. I leaned down and scooped up some cool water, splashing it on my face and neck. You'd never think a war was waging on this hot summer day, not too far away from this quiet pond. I'd just come from Farmers Mills where the air buzzed with talk of danger. As I brushed wisps of hair away from my face, the sound of hoofbeats startled me. I turned to see two rough looking men barreling down the road toward me. I didn't recognize them and I knew most everyone around here because my father was a colonel in the militia. These men had to be Skinners. Skinners steal anything valuable and sell it to the British.

"A beautiful horse you have there," one of the men said as he came to an abrupt halt. He dismounted and started toward me down the bank that led to the water's edge. He was tall and lanky. His beard was spattered with tobacco and bits of food. His eyes leered at me and his mouth twisted into a wry grin. "You'll be giving him to us to help the British fight this war against the rebel colonists."

"Sorry you'll have to walk home miss," the second man said as he too dismounted at the top of the rise.

"I see you two are brave fighting men, picking on an innocent girl to take her horse and make her walk home," I said as I gathered Star's reins and drew him around between the two men and me.

The first man dropped his horse's reins and took a few steps closer.

My heart pounded, my chest tightened, and I couldn't breathe. I gathered my skirts, stuffed my foot in the stirrup and leapt into the saddle. Kicking my heels into Star's flanks I urged him up the bank and into a gallop. I heard the men swear as they mounted their horses and started after me. Could we outrun them? I wasn't sure but no one would take my horse as long as I could do anything about it.

Glancing back over my shoulder I could see through the dust that the Skinners weren't far behind. If we could get to the woods, maybe I could lose them. I could feel Star's strong stride under me as the wind cooled my hot face. We cut across the first field and raced toward the gate. I knew Star could jump it because we had done it many times for fun. On the other side of that field was the deep forest that butted up to our orchard. Over the gate we sailed and galloped on. Reaching the edge of the forest at last, I reined Star into a trot as we slipped into the protection of the woods.

A LETTER FROM FATHER
Chapter Two
1776, 25 August

I looked back but I couldn't see the Skinners. The forest was silent. I had lost them. As Star and I made our way home, I felt guilty at the thought of what could have happened. I should have come directly back the way Mother told me but I couldn't help myself. The afternoon was so beautiful that I stopped at White Pond so Star could have a drink. I never get to have time alone because all the children need my attention. There are seven of them besides me and since I'm the oldest, Mother expects me to do everything. This adventure would be my secret, even from Rebecca. I bedded Star and scurried to the house. I was late and I knew it.

"Sybil, where have you been?" Mother asked as I slid into the kitchen still out of breath. "Tell your brothers to tend to the animals and then come in to help me with supper."

I groaned under my breath. I'd just outrun the Skinners but I couldn't tell her about that so I stomped out of the kitchen and headed for the front of the house. Out on the porch I watched my brothers Archibald and Derick chase Henry out of the trees. Archibald caught up with Henry, knocked him down, and stuck his foot on Henry's back.

"Throw down your weapon, you dirty British scoundrel!" he

shouted. "We'll send you back where you came from!"

Derick grabbed a stick out of Henry's hand and pointed it at him as if it were a gun. They were playing, but I knew the real war was going on not far from here. Father was there and I wanted to be there too, but this war was men's doings. Why couldn't women help too? It didn't seem fair.

"Archibald, stop that!" I yelled. "Put down those sticks and go feed the animals. You know Mother doesn't like you to play war."

Henry popped up, grabbed the stick from Derick, and took off running toward the barn. With their heads down, Archibald and Derick ambled after him. I turned, went into the house, and began setting the table.

#

When we finished the dishes, and Baby Abigail and Tertullus were in bed, the rest of us gathered to listen to Mother read Father's letter.

1776, 20 August   *North Castle*

My dear Abigail and loving children,

I hope this letter finds you all in good health and spirits. I regret to tell you that I will not be coming home now. I am sending this letter by special messenger for fear that it will be intercepted. Now that the Patriots have signed a Declaration of Independence the battles have become more intense. The news from the front lines is not encouraging.

The British have pushed General Washington's troops

north to White Plains. Last night we moved the 7th Regiment of the militia to fortify the higher hills near North Castle and I have been ordered by General Washington to remain.

Here we will set up a defense of the Hudson Highlands. My fondest hope is to keep the perils of war away from our precious valley.

I was able to promote the capable Captain Robinson to major and because I trust his leadership, I may take my leave in mid September.

I remain your loving husband and father,

Henry

"Sybil, do you think Father is shooting all those British soldiers?" asked Archibald.

"I hope not," I said, "but war is dangerous you know and Father and his troops are trying to protect our homes, and us."

"Hush," Mother said. " I don't want to hear any more about war. It's time for all you children to get to bed. Sybil, help the younger ones get settled and let's have no more of that talk."

I held my tongue. Mother was right. How could I tell a ten-year-old about the massacre in Boston, the British invasion of New York, and the killing and burning of people's homes? Mother and Father kept news of the war and the brutality from me too, but I listened whenever adults talked. The British were retaliating after some men in Boston threw a shipment of tea into the harbor. They want to control us and tax our imports so it's tearing apart our country. Some of our neighbors, whom we have known for a long time, are Loyalists. Others, like our family, have taken up the Patriot cause. You can't tell one from the other, so no one can be trusted.

Shaking my head, I chased these thoughts away. Father was gone and I was stuck helping Mother. Tomorrow, like every August, I had to make candles with the children to get ready for winter.

THE MISHAP
Chapter Three
1776, 26 August

I woke with a start. The cool morning air drifted into my open window reminding me that fall and winter were on the way. Slipping out of bed, I took care not to wake Rebecca. I made my way downstairs to get ready for the long day ahead. Mother wasn't up so I assumed she went back to bed after feeding Baby Abigail. She was tired and cranky all the time.

I started the fire and set up two large kettles half-filled with water to melt the tallow. In the shed I put up the poles to hold the candle-rods. After that I went upstairs to wake up the children.

"Rebecca, wake up. We're making candles," I said shaking her shoulder.

"Do we have to do it today?" she asked groaning as she slid her feet over the edge of the bed. I ignored her.

"You too, Mary," I said. "You're old enough to tie the wicks."

The three of us dressed in our everyday dresses and stockings. I brushed Mary's hair and plaited it in one braid down her back. Rebecca and I did the same, but we pinned ours up, wanting to look older. Mother hadn't objected. We donned our mobcaps and tied our aprons and I went across the hall to wake the boys.

"Archibald! Henry! Derick! Wake up!" I called. "Time to do

chores. You get no help from us this morning because we are making candles."

"How unfair!" Archibald answered back. Bare feet echoed as they hit the wood floor.

"Hush, you'll wake Mother," I hissed. "All you ever do is complain. This is a family and we all have to do our part. If you're quick, I'll fix some johnnycakes to go with your breakfast."

I wondered when I had started to sound like Mother.

After breakfast the boys went out to the barn. Rebecca stirred the hot tallow and I set the moulds out for pouring.

"Mary, start tying the wicks," I said. "Tie the ones in these moulds first then the ones on the sticks. Rebecca and I will be ready to pour soon."

"You're bossy," Mary said as she began to tie one end of a wick to a small piece of wire and placed it over a mould.

"Pull it tight so the wick hangs straight down the middle of the mould," I told her.

"You don't have to tell me. I'm old enough to do this, remember?" Mary said.

Soon all the molds were filled and cooling in the shed.

"Where are the boys?" I asked.

"They're probably playing," said Rebecca. "I'll go see what they're up to."

"No need," said Archibald, bounding into the kitchen followed by Henry and Derick.

"Watch what you're doing," I said, as Archibald bumped into the kettle with the hot tallow. It slopped out over the side and into the fire. I jumped back and gasped for breath. Flames lapped at the top of the hearth leaving big black fingers on the brick. My eyes started to water as an acrid smell rose up in the smoke. Rebecca, Mary, and the two little boys started to scream. Was the house going to go up in smoke before my eyes? I steadied my thoughts and scooped up some sand from the bucket we kept near the hearth and threw it on the flames. Grabbing some more I threw it again. The hissing stopped and the flames died. I let out my breath.

"Did the flames get you?" I asked Rebecca.

"No, they startled me that's all."

"How about the rest of you?"

"We're fine," the boys and Mary answered in chorus.

I looked around at the telltale signs of our accident and sighed. I'd have to do a lot of scrubbing to get those marks off the hearth.

"We can't afford to lose any more tallow. Mother will blame me. All of you must be more careful when you're dipping. Come on now, let's get started"

"Derick will get in the way if he helps," said Henry.

"Not if you show him what to do," I replied.

The three boys and Mary dipped the wicks into the hot tallow and walked them to the poles in the shed. There they hung them between two poles to cool before the next trip to the dipping kettle. Around and around they went as the candles got thicker and thicker. We were almost finished when Mother came in from working in the garden with Tertullus and Baby Abigail.

"How are the candles?" she asked. "What's that smell? How did all that charring get on the mantle?"

"We had a slight accident," I said. "I took care of it."

"You have to be more careful, Sybil," Mother replied. "We can't have you burning down the house."

I turned away so Mother wouldn't see my face.

THE THIEVES
Chapter Four
1776, 7 September

A week later, Rebecca and I were trudging along the road to the gristmill. The crisp morning air of September surrounded us and the red, yellow, and orange leaves sparkled in the sun. I loved this time of year.

"Hello girls," Mr. Kent said with a big smile as we approached. "I've got a special favor to ask you today. Can you two ride to Farmers Mills and put up these broadsides to let the farmers know the mill is open and operating?"

"I'm not sure that Mother will let us, but we'll ask," I replied.

Mr. Kent gave us the broadsides. We turned around and ran home, bursting into the kitchen where Mother was making bread.

"Mother, Mr. Kent wants us to put up these broadsides telling about our services here at the mill," I said. "Can we ride to Farmers Mills and take them?"

I would do anything to get away for an afternoon.

"Too dangerous," said Mother. "Just last night, those thieving Skinners robbed three horses from the Brewster farm and burned the barn. They may still be in the neighborhood."

I said nothing about meeting the Skinners myself. Certainly if Mother knew she would never let us go.

"Mr. Kent says most of the young men who are not old enough to enlist in the militia are doing the heavy work at the mill. He can't spare them for a ride to Farmers Mills. The broadsides must go up to let the farmers know we are running," I argued.

Mother sighed. "Fine," she said at last, "but be sure to stay on the main road so you will be safe."

I packed some fresh bread and dried meat for our lunch, and Rebecca saddled up Star and Blackie. We took the broadsides and started out on the road to Farmers Mills.

The day had warmed and I felt free at last from the demands of chores and children.

"We should ride around White Pond because the trip will be faster," I suggested.

"I don't think that's a good idea," said Rebecca. "What about the Skinners?"

"No one will even see us once we get into the woods. If the Skinners were there they're probably gone by now. They don't stay around after they steal something. They ride off and sell what they have stolen to the British. I'm not afraid of Skinners," I said, squaring my shoulders and lifting my chin. "We'll turn off at the Indian path just up ahead."

The damp forest air hit our faces as we left the hot dusty road. The sun flickered through the trees leaving patches of shadow on the soft forest floor. Robins and jays called high up in the trees. Once in a while a squirrel or chipmunk would cross our path and the horses would shy a little. We came to the outlet of the pond and traveled along the edge looking for a place to cross. Just as we crossed the stream and started up a small rise, we heard voices and horses whinnying. A glow of a campfire shone between the trees.

"Get down from your horse," I whispered to Rebecca as I dismounted.

"I told you we might run into those thieves if we took this shorter route. What do we do now?" Rebecca whispered back.

"We'll just have to walk the horses further into the woods and hope they don't catch us," I said.

"You got us into this mess," said Rebecca, scowling. "We should have stayed on the main road like Mother told us."

"Hush, and just keep going," I hissed back.

We picked our way quietly through the brush keeping one hand on our horses' noses so they wouldn't whinny and give us away. We could hear the men laughing and talking.

"Had a good night last night," I heard one of the men say.

"We sure will get a lot from the British for these horses," said another.

"Those Patriot sympathizers are easy pickings," said the first man. "I loved seeing their barn go up in flames. They should know enough to side with the British."

Slowly we made our way around the Skinners. At first the going was easy. Then Star stepped on a large branch and it snapped with a retort that sounded like a musket. We stopped dead and waited.

"Did you hear that?" one man asked.

"Hear what?" another answered.

"Sounded like someone over there," the first man retorted.

"You're just hearing things. Did last night's adventure rattle your brain? No one is out here."

I could hear Rebecca breathing beside me. I realized I'd been holding my breath. Slowly I let it out. We didn't move. We just waited and listened. Those Skinners must be lazy or tired, I thought. No one came and nothing happened so after a few minutes we continued.

When we reached Farmers Mills we posted our broadsides on trees and buildings in the village.

"We're done," I said.

"Should we go to the store and see if we can find someone to tell about the Skinners?" Rebecca asked.

"No, the men have all gone to the front. Let's head home. Rebecca, you must swear not to tell Mother about our adventure. "

"Why should I?" Rebecca said laughing. "Have you been up to something, Sybil?

"None of your business. Now swear."

I didn't tell her how much I wished I could be with Father and help with the war or how tedious my life seemed. What was wrong with wanting a little adventure?

"I swear," she replied and we both mounted up and headed back home by the main road.

FATHER'S HOMECOMING
Chapter Five
1776, 15 September

Every afternoon I sat down with the older children and gave them their lessons. The weather was like summer as it often is in mid-September, so we chose to sit on the piazza. We had only two hornbooks, a Bible, and a new novel called *Robinson Crusoe*, which was given to us by Mr. Jay, a friend of Father's. Archibald was reciting his numbers when we saw three men on horseback galloping up the road. I ran and grabbed the musket from the corner where we kept it. The children crouched down under the table.

"Come quick! Come quick!" shouted a man I had never seen before.

I lifted the musket to my waist and said nothing. As they neared the house, I could see that they were leading a horse whose rider was slumped over his saddle.

"Hurry, it's Colonel Ludington! He's been hit," the other man said, jumping from his horse and running to help the wounded soldier. I couldn't believe it. Father had been shot! Was he dying? How bad was it? I handed the musket to Rebecca and ran to Father. Seeing me, Father struggled to sit up. I gasped when I saw his blood making a large stain on the shoulder of his jacket.

"I only have a superficial wound in my shoulder," Father said.

"Go get your mother and she will fix me up as good as new."

"Mary, go get Mother while the soldier and I help Father!" I shouted.

Slowly Father dismounted as we guided him to the ground. I grabbed his good arm, swung it over my back, and put my arm around his waist. He groaned as the soldier did the same with his wounded arm. We made our way up the steps and settled him in a chair.

"Oh Henry, what happened?" Mother cried as she rushed out the front door, handed Baby Abigail to me, and flung herself at Father.

"Nothing that a little of your home cooking and special herbs won't cure," Father said. "We are doing such a good job protecting the Highlands that General Howe has put a price on my head. I think I was grazed by a bullet from a Loyalist who was trying to collect the ransom."

"Take him inside," Mother said.

The two soldiers helped Father into the parlor where he stretched out on the settee.

"Rebecca, make your father some sassafras tea," Mother said. "Get some wild ginger and juniper berries and add them to it. Mary, take Baby Abigail and Tertullus upstairs. They're too young to see this. Boys, take the muskets and go outside to keep watch. Sybil and I will dress Father's wound. Now get along, all of you."

I'd never heard Mother bark orders like that before. Mary took Baby Abigail and I hurried to the kitchen. I brought back a bowl of water from the kettle and a clean piece of lint. Mother began to cleanse Father's wound while I fetched some oil and clean lint for a dressing. I dipped the lint in the oil and a mild digestive that we kept for wounds and hurried back to the parlor.

"Father," I asked, "are you sure a bullet isn't inside your shoulder?"

"Yes Sybil, I'll be fine."

"Henry, I've been so worried about you," Mother said. "Are you going to stay home until your wound heals?"

"Of course, my dear," Father said. "The men must return to North Castle tonight and report. I will rest here for a few weeks and then I must return and give Major Robinson an opportunity to visit his family."

THE RUSE
Chapter Six
1776, 15 September

Father was home at last. But was he safe? And what about us? Would someone try to collect the ransom for Father's head again? Would they succeed the next time? I could feel my stomach churn at the thought of Father lying dead in some deserted forest or on the battlefield.

When his wound was dressed and he had finished Rebecca's tea, I watched Father fall into a deep sleep. Mother fed Baby Abigail and began to make the evening meal. When I heard her clatter I rose quietly and went to help. We ate heartily and after supper, Rebecca and I went back out on the piazza to stand guard. Our muskets across our laps, we sat stiffly in our chairs, looking out over the road and the woods beyond.

We must have dozed off because I was awakened by a rustling noise and the call of an owl.

"Rebecca," I whispered, "did you hear that?"

"I didn't hear anything," Rebecca said, rubbing her eyes. "You must have been dreaming."

"No, I wasn't. There it goes again."

"I heard it that time," Rebecca said. "Someone's moving. They're coming toward the house."

"I see them too," I whispered. "Is it the Skinners or someone coming for Father? I can't tell. We have to go inside and wake him. They're surrounding the house."

Quietly we let ourselves in the front door and crept over to where Father lay sleeping.

"Father," I whispered in his ear. "I think some men are surrounding the house. They could be after you."

Father woke up with a jolt.

"What Sybil? You think what?"

"I said Rebecca and I saw some men surrounding the house."

Father moaned as he rose and staggered over to the window.

"Do you girls have your muskets? Looks like a band of Loyalists and not our own militia. I think I recognize a few of them. Get your mother and wake the boys and Mary," he said. "I have an idea that might just keep them from coming in. We need my jackets and all of our hats. Go quickly now."

Rebecca and I ran upstairs and woke everyone. We fetched the jackets and hats and returned to the parlor.

"Abigail," Father said to Mother, "light as many candles as you can all around the house. Children, dress in my jackets and take turns walking back and forth in front of all the windows. Sybil, you put one of my jackets on Tertullus, and Henry, you carry him on your shoulders. Archibald, you do the same and put Derick on your shoulders. Sybil, you and Rebecca put on jackets and hats and start walking. Maybe we can convince the intruders that we have many men in the house."

We scrambled to get ready. Dressed in Father's jackets, we walked through the front rooms nodding to each other as if we were talking. Taking turns to rest, we sat in the straight chairs around the dinning room table and pretended to have a refreshing drink. Back and forth, round and round, we went until the wee hours of the morning hoping our charade would work. Maybe the intruders would think Father came home with a band of men and not with just the two who had already returned to camp.

When the first rays of sunlight peaked through our parlor window and Baby Abigail began to cry for her morning feeding, Rebecca and I crept back out on the porch with our muskets. The intruders were gone but their footprints covered the wet grass. We resumed our watch while the other children fell into bed exhausted.

SOMEONE NEW
Chapter Seven
1776, 3 October

The Committee for Detecting and Defeating Conspiracies was meeting at our house again in the west parlor. When I entered with a tray filled with applesauce cake and cider, I saw someone new. He was younger than the rest, and really quite dashing. I lifted my hand to push a wisp of hair out of my face and almost dropped the tray. His features were not what made me notice him although his nose was prominent and his forehead high. It was his eyes. They shone with adventure and laughter. His wide smile revealed white teeth. He winked at me. He was dressed in a waistcoat, vest, and a clean shirt, but his boots were covered with mud. As I set the heavy tray full of cake and the tin mugs down on the table my hands shook so the mugs nearly toppled over.

"Gentlemen, you remember my daughter, Sybil," Father said. "And Sybil, I think you know everyone but our newcomer, Mr. Enoch Crosby. Come over here and meet him."

I could feel my face getting red and my hands were damp from pouring the cold cider. I walked over and curtsied, not daring to look up. Surely he would notice my awkwardness. I wished I had pinned my long braid up onto my head. I must look like a child.

"I am very glad to meet you," Mr. Crosby said. "You can call me

Enoch, if you wish."

I was tongue-tied and didn't say a word. I usually call all Father's friends mister or sir. I didn't get the chance to meet many young men and I didn't know what to make of him.

"Sybil, please sit down and stay," Father said. "If we need anything else, you can fetch it for us."

I sat down in the straight chair in the corner and looked at Enoch Crosby. I didn't listen to the business until he began to talk.

"I'm here today at the request of Esquire Young to tell you my story," Enoch began. "It all started in August after I enlisted again into the regiment commanded by Colonel Sworthaut. I was late and the regiment had already left Fredricksburg, so I decided to continue on alone."

"Were you aware of the dangers?" asked one of the men as he reached over to help himself to another piece of cake.

"Certainly sir," Enoch replied, "but it seemed to be the best course of action at the time."

Enoch turned, glanced at me, and turned back. He did it so quickly, I wasn't sure it really happened. I looked over at Father. Did he see Enoch look at me?

"Where did you get the information about the company that was raising men to help the British?" Father asked.

"Just before I reached Pines Bridge I ran into a stranger who accosted me and demanded to know if I was going down to join the British," Enoch continued. "I said yes. Since I had been mistaken for a Loyalist, I kept up the ruse to see what would happen next. Feeling surer of me, the man finally told me his name was Bunker. I asked if he knew a way I could get there safely. He was so certain that I intended to join the British, he told me about a company that was raising troops in that neighborhood," Enoch said.

While Enoch was talking, I watched as his face lit up. Excitement radiated from him and I couldn't keep my eyes off him. He looked back at me and his eyes met mine. He smiled. I smiled back.

"What are the names of those scoundrels?" Mr. Jay asked.

"The captain is called Fowler and the lieutenant, Kipp," Enoch said. "Once I had learned this I told Mr. Bunker I did not want to wait but would continue on alone. I left him and traveled on until nightfall, arriving at Esquire Young's house. He put me up for the night and sent me to report my findings to this committee."

"What is your trade, sir?" Father asked.

"I'm a shoemaker," Enoch said. "Before joining the regiment, I traveled around this area searching for shoes to repair. I know the area well which is why I was able to find Esquire Young's house."

"Mr. Crosby, will you retire to the east parlor while we discuss your situation?" Father asked.

"Certainly sir," Enoch replied and got to his feet. "Sybil, will you escort me?"

"Of course," I mumbled as I stood up and began walking toward the door in a daze. Enoch put his hand on my back to guide me through. This was the first time I noticed a man's touch. My face got hot and I was afraid to look his way. When we crossed the hall into the east parlor, I was relieved to see Mother there with all the children. In a short time Father came back to fetch Mr. Crosby.

"Well, sir," Father said with his jovial laugh, "you can come back and we'll discuss our plan with you."

They started back to the west parlor and I followed. I went

quickly to the tray and filled it with the cups and leftover cake.

"We will send you to Captain Townsend," Father continued. He will keep you as a prisoner. You can feign escape and return to Mr. Bunker to continue the ruse until the Loyalists are captured."

That's all I heard as I shut the door and took the tray back to the kitchen. I thought about him that night before I fell asleep, wondering if he would be safe.

TARGET PRACTICE
Chapter Eight
1776, 16 October

With Father home our family life had returned to normal. The mill was running smoothly and messengers rode in daily bringing news from North Castle. I didn't see Enoch again, but Father conducted the business of the Committee on Safety from our house.

The five children and I walked to the orchard carrying baskets for the apples to finish the last of the harvesting. Mother made us take two of the muskets with us when we went to the orchard because she couldn't see us from the house. I carried one of them and Rebecca carried the other. The boys begged over and over to carry them but I said no. Attached to my apron strings I carried the bullets in a pouch. This morning I let Archibald carry the powder horn so he would keep quiet.

"Come on, Sybil. How do you expect me to be as good a shot as you are if I never get a chance to shoot?" Archibald asked.

"Don't you ever stop complaining?" I replied. "If we get most of the apples picked, maybe we will have time for some target shooting. I think it's time we taught Henry to shoot."

"I promise I will dig all the bullets out of the trees if we can practice," said Archibald.

"I want to learn to shoot now," declared Henry.

"You'll have to wait and see if we have time," I told him. "We're almost there and if you all work hard we should be done in a few hours."

We reached the orchard and put some of the baskets under the first tree. Rebecca and I leaned the muskets against the tree and Archibald hesitated before he put the powder horn down next to them. Archibald, Henry, and Derick climbed the trees and tossed the last of the ripe apples down to Mary and Rebecca. The girls caught them in their aprons and put them into the baskets. I sat under the first tree on a big rock and kept watch. Someone always had to keep watch because the Skinners robbed people whenever they could now.

"Sybil, we're almost finished. Can't we practice shooting now?" Archibald begged.

"I don't see why not," I replied as they all came over to where I was sitting. "What will we use as a target?" Archibald asked. "Maybe that big oak tree."

"Then we would lose too many bullets into the woods with Henry learning to shoot," I said. "I think we should stay in the orchard and use one of the apple trees. That way we will have a better chance of finding the lead from the bullets."

"We won't be really shooting unless we shoot into the woods," Archibald said. "Do you think soldiers and Skinners shoot in apple orchards?"

"OK, but you must make a real effort to aim. We can't lose too much of Father's ammunition," I said. "Let's move closer so you can aim at the big oak."

"Can I shoot first since the guns are already loaded?" asked Archibald.

"Yes, and then you will explain to Henry how to load the gun safely," I said.

We all walked over to a spot about a hundred feet from the big tree. Rebecca and I carried the muskets, their barrels pointing safely toward the ground. When we reached the correct distance, Archibald went down on one knee and waited patiently for me to hand him the musket. I handed him the musket, he took aim, and shot toward the tree. Mary and Derick covered their ears.

"I hit the tree!" Archibald shouted as he handed me the musket and ran to find the bullet. I watched him dig the lead out of the tree with his knife.

"See, I told you I would be able to dig it out!" he yelled.

"Get back here and let me see you show Henry how to load the musket," I said, as Archibald scurried back to where we stood.

"Pay attention Henry. You pour the powder down the barrel, but not too much. Then you drop in the ball and use a bit of this paper for the wadding. Ram all of it down, putting the gun stock of the musket on the ground. Be sure to point the barrel away from everyone."

Archibald quickly went down on one knee, lifted the musket, and got ready to shoot.

"It's my turn to try," Henry said.

"Quiet. Look, there is a wild turkey over there," hissed Archibald. "I'll get him for our supper. Won't Mother be surprised?"

Archibald aimed and shot. The turkey dropped. Suddenly from the far end of the field two men came galloping at full tilt. From this distance they looked like the same two men I had met on the way home from Farmers Mills. When they came to the turkey, one of the men jumped down from his horse and scooped up Archibald's turkey.

"Thanks for a delicious supper," he yelled as they galloped off.

"But that was ours," said Archibald. "Those nasty Skinners must have heard us shooting. They should mind their own business and do their own hunting."

"Not much we can do about it now," I said. "At least they didn't take our apples. Let's get home now in case there are any other dangers lurking out here."

OFF TO MARKET
Chapter Nine
1776, 23 October

"Sybil, can you come here?" asked Father after supper. "I need you to go to Fishkill tomorrow to deliver some bread and dried meat to the Loyalist prisoners who are being held in the old stone church in the center of town. You will be carrying a letter for the young man you met a while ago."

"You mean Enoch Crosby?" I asked, hoping Father wouldn't see the redness creeping up my face. I turned away, fiddling with my apron.

"Yes, that's who I mean," said Father. "He must escape and return here for the committee meeting in three days."

"But how will I get a letter to him? Do you think I can get into the church with the prisoners?"

"Sybil, you are a smart girl and a pretty one too. I think you can figure out a way to meet up with Enoch and give him our message. The message will be in code so if it is intercepted you won't be harmed," Father explained. "Come on over here and watch me compose it."

I went over to the desk and watched Father dip his quill into the ink and begin to write. His penmanship was perfect and I watched him write a short note.

My Dear Sir:

I am sorry that I must inform you that your cousin must leave tonight because of illness in the family. I am hopeful that you will come back to Ludington's as soon as possible. Give my best regards to the family.

Truly yours,

Henry

Father then took a little funny shaped piece of parchment out of his vest pocket and placed it over the letter. The letter then read: "Leave tonight come back to Ludington's." I couldn't believe my eyes.

"Does that mean that Enoch will be coming back here?" I asked.

"He has important information to report to the committee," said Father. "You must be sure to deliver this letter. He carries a piece of parchment just like this one so he will be able to decipher the message."

Before going to bed I stitched a small pocket in the hem of my long skirt. While I was sewing my mind whirled. Would Enoch remember me? Was he safe? What would I say to him? The dangers of my mission lurked in my mind but Father had trusted me for the first time. I would be doing something for the Patriot cause and I wouldn't let him down. I slipped the letter into the pocket and basted it closed.

The next morning when I came down for breakfast, the kitchen smelled of baked bread. Mother had been up all night baking small loaves for me to take to the prisoners.

"You and Rebecca will take the wagon today and go to Fishkill to do the marketing," said Mother. "You will also deliver these breads and some of this dried meat to the prisoners being held in the old stone church. Rebecca will wait in the wagon while you talk to Captain Townsend. You should have no trouble getting him to let you deliver the breads to each of the thirty men."

Will Captain Townsend be there waiting for us, I wondered. How would I slip the note to Enoch? I was surprised to see Mother had packed the thirty small loaves of bread into two large baskets. Would Rebecca realize what I was really doing? Would I be getting both of us into danger? I harnessed Father's black stallion to the wagon and Rebecca helped me load the two baskets. As we started out, I looked back over my shoulder. Father stood with his arm around Mother's shoulders watching us leave. My heart jumped into my throat and tears filled my eyes. I'm doing this for my family, I thought.

THE PRISONERS
Chapter Ten
1776, 24 October

We arrived in Fishkill about noon. Father had insisted I pack the musket under the wagon seat just in case we should meet some Skinners, but our trip was uneventful.

Mother asked us to visit the dry goods store and pick up some material she had ordered. She was planning to make some new dresses and hats for us girls. Rebecca and I had just packed the material into the wagon when we heard a big commotion coming from the old stone church.

"You men move right along there!" yelled one of the guards. "If you don't, I'll shoot you for treason. I'll never understand why you don't side with the Patriots. What's so great about those British oppressors anyway?" He fired his musket up into the air for effect. Both Rebecca and I ducked down behind the wagon.

I mustered up my courage, leaped up, and grabbed one of the baskets of bread.

"Rebecca, you get up on the wagon seat and wait for me. I am going to try to deliver these breads," I whispered and took off running.

I approached the guard and curtsied.

"Excuse me, sir. Is Captain Townsend around?" I asked. "My father, Colonel Ludington, and his family have sent these breads and some dried meat to help feed the prisoners. May I see him please?"

"He's not here," the guard replied.

My heart sank. How was I going to get to see Enoch and give him my message? I looked around and saw him about three quarters of the way down the line. He looked bedraggled and worn. Life for him must have been hard since I'd last seen him. My heart started to beat so fast I thought the guard might hear it.

"I will just hand out these breads when the prisoners walk by if that is fine with you sir," I said.

"Sure lass, I can see no harm in that," he said and started poking the nearest prisoner with his bayonet. "Come on you traitors; come get yourselves a bite to eat. This may be your last meal for a long time."

I set down the basket and began to unwrap the bread. Carefully, I handed each man a loaf and a little of the dried meat. Soon the basket was empty.

"Excuse me sir," I said to the guard. "I must return to my wagon and get the other basket."

Enoch had gotten close enough to see me. I looked up and his eyes met mine. I felt a blush creep up my neck and warm my cheeks.

"Sir," I said to the guard, "my wagon is just over there. Can you have one of the prisoners help me with the other basket? It is much heavier than the first one."

"I'd be happy to help the lady," said Enoch. "Certainly you can trust me not to run away, sir, and the lady looks tired after handing out all those provisions."

"Go ahead, but mind you don't do anything out of the ordinary or I'll have a good excuse to shoot you," said the guard.

I picked up the basket and Enoch took my arm. He was such a

gentleman that I could feel my face getting hot all over again. We made our way down the road to the wagon. I lifted the empty basket inside, took the full basket, and placed it at my feet. Then I leaned over and pretended to fix my shoe but instead I slipped the note out of the secret pocket and held it in my palm. As Enoch reached for the basket I felt his hand touch mine. My skin burned as the note passed between us. He looked at me and smiled.

We both started back to the line of prisoners. Putting the heavy basket on the ground he stepped into his place in line. I resumed handing out the food and when Enoch's turn came, I felt his eyes boring into mine. Flustered, I dropped his bread onto the dusty road.

"I'm sorry sir," I stammered, feeling as if I would faint.

"No problem," he said with a smile. "I'll just dust it off and it will be fine."

When the bread and dried meat were gone, I turned and made my way back to the wagon. I climbed up and sat heavily on the seat.

"What was that all about?" said Rebecca. "Wasn't that Mr. Crosby, the man at Father's last meeting? The one you were so smitten with, Sybil."

"You hush up Rebecca. What do you know anyway?" I shot back.

The wind had started to blow and rain pelted down on us as we started back home. Rebecca and I didn't talk. She would never understand how much I wanted to help the Patriot cause. Only boys were allowed to help and it just didn't seem fair. We drove in silence for the next two hours and arrived home in time for supper.

Later, Father called me aside as I was going upstairs to bed.

"How was your trip to Fishkill?" he asked.

"I gave Enoch the letter," I replied. "I just can't help wondering if he will make it back to our house considering the weather and the danger."

"Don't worry about him," Father said. "He's been in more difficult situations than this. That man can talk his way out of anything. Goodnight, Sybil, and thank you. You have been a great help today."

As I dozed off, I couldn't help thinking about Enoch.

THE MIDNIGHT VISITOR
Chapter Eleven
1776, 26 October

Each week, Rebecca and I had been taking turns keeping watch at night. Since the cold fall days were fast approaching, I slept on the settee in the west parlor, fully dressed with the musket next to me on the floor. Ever since our trip to Fishkill, I could not help thinking about Enoch. Would he get away safely? Was he thinking of me? Had I led him into grave danger? I was just dozing off when I heard a rustling on the porch. Was it the wind causing the bushes to scrape the porch railing? I swung my feet on to the floor and stood up without making a sound, grabbed the musket, and crawled over to the window to peek out. A full moon hung in the darkness like a silver ball. A few clouds floated across its face obscuring my view. I heard the noise again on my left. Turning, I saw a man climbing up the wide front steps. He was hunched over against the wind, his hat pulled down, and his face partially visible. I slid over to the door and I pushed down on the latch. The door swung open and I stepped out onto the piazza holding the loaded musket to my shoulder.

"Who goes there?" I demanded in a harsh whisper. "Identify yourself now!"

"Enoch Crosby, to see Colonel Ludington," the man said as he looked up to show me his face.

I sighed in relief and began to blush. I was glad the darkness hid my feelings so well.

"Come in out of the cold, and I will go fetch Father," I said, stepping aside so he could enter. I closed the door and went to wake Father. I tapped on Father's door.

"What is it?" Father's sleepy voice replied.

"Enoch Crosby escaped and has just arrived. I told him to wait while I came to fetch you."

"Take him to the kitchen, stoke the fire, and brew him some sassafras tea," Father said. I could hear him as he began to get dressed.

I went back to the front hall and invited our guest into the kitchen. After lighting a few candles, I stoked the fire. The coals were still hot from supper and the tinder I threw on them burst into flame. I ladled some water from the drinking bucket into a kettle and set it over the fire to boil.

"We meet again," said Enoch.

I didn't dare look at him so I busied myself with the tin mugs. Taking out some of yesterday's bread, some butter, and a new crock of jam, I set them in front of Enoch. Then I took the boiling water and poured it into the mug. Using my apron to hold the mug since the handle was hot, I placed it in front of the disheveled man.

"This should warm you up," I said at last. The silence hung between us like humidity on a hot day.

"It looks wonderful and I have traveled a long way," said Enoch. "I've had to come by circular routes, and travel by night."

"How long did it take you to get here?" I asked to keep him talking. I loved watching his eyes light up and his face shine as he spoke.

"Much longer than it should have," he replied taking another piece of bread and slathering it with jam. "I finally acquired a horse from a Mister Kent. My saddle bag with supplies for repairing shoes weighed me down so I welcomed the horse for the last few miles of the trip. This food tastes wonderful. The last thing I had to eat was the loaf of bread and dried meat you gave me."

"I'm so sorry," I said. "I didn't realize how hungry you were. Can I fix you some dried meat and cheese?"

"That would sure go down well," Enoch said. He picked up his tea and took three long swigs.

I fetched some dried ham and some of Father's favorite cheese and placed it on the table in front of Enoch. I got him a knife and fork and placed them on either side of his plate. As I did this he looked up and gave me a wide smile.

"Well there young man, hope my daughter has served you everything you need," said Father as he came stomping into the kitchen and slapped Enoch on the back. "Glad to see you've made it here, just in time for the meeting of the committee tomorrow night. Can you get me a spot of that sassafras tea, Sybil?"

Father sat down and I served him a tin mug filled with tea.

"Mr. Crosby, may I fill your cup again?" I asked.

"Yes, please. I thought I told you to call me Enoch," he said finishing up the last of his bread and cheese.

I turned and started wrapping up the bread so Enoch and Father wouldn't notice my rosy cheeks.

"Well, Enoch," said Father. "We shall retire to the west parlor and I can hear what you have to say. Then you can bed down on the settee there for the rest of the night. Sybil, you can go up to your own room. Enoch will sleep here to stand guard."

I hoped the disappointment I felt didn't show on my face. I wanted to hear the details of Enoch's escape and his journey to our house. I picked up the cups and plates and set them on the counter to be washed in the morning with the breakfast dishes. I put away the bread, cheese, and dried meat and crept up the stairs to my room. I could hear the two men talking but couldn't make out what they were saying. Finally, I must have dozed off.

THE SPY
Chapter Twelve
1776, 27 October

"Sybil, Sybil," said Archibald as he bounded up the stairs into the hall. "There's a strange horse tethered to the tree in front of the house. I saw it from my window. Who is here? What's going on?"

"One of Father's friends arrived in the night and will be staying until the committee meets here tomorrow night," I said. "Stop making a racket or you will wake the others. It's still early yet. Since you have so much energy, why don't you take his horse out to the barn, brush him, and bed him down with some food?"

I could hear Archibald take the stairs two at a time. He certainly had enthusiasm when he wanted to do something. I dressed, being sure to pin my hair up today. I put on a fresh apron and picked my prettiest mobcap. I slipped downstairs to begin the morning chores. When I went to the kitchen I jumped in surprise. There at the table where he had sat the night before was Enoch.

"Good morning sir," I said.

"May I help you bring in some wood for the fire and water from the well?" he asked. "And I thought I told you to call me Enoch. There is no reason to be so formal Sybil. I can call you Sybil, can't I?"

"That's fine," I said and handed him the bucket. "The well is out the back to the right of the house. Thank you."

Enoch swooped up the bucket and sauntered out the door. As I had done the night before, I threw tinder on the coals and the fire sprang up. There were two logs left in the wood box in the corner of the kitchen and I laid them carefully on the fire. I had no sooner started the water for tea, when the children came pounding into the kitchen. You can count on Archibald to get everyone up if he wakes up early.

"Who is here?" Henry asked.

"Who owns this hat?" asked Derick.

"Mother's feeding Baby Abigail," said Rebecca as she entered with Mary who was holding Tertullus' hand.

"You all sit down now and put on your best manners," I said.

Just then Enoch stepped through the door with a bucket of fresh drinking water.

"Where would you like this?" he asked in his deep voice.

"At the side of the sink," I replied. "You remember the others. Please sit down and I will fix breakfast."

"Make johnnycakes please, Sybil," said Archibald as he rushed into the kitchen. "I got that horse all settled in and now I'm hungry. Oh, excuse me, sir. Good morning."

The children all sat down around the table and fixed their eyes on Enoch. He smiled and looked from one to the other.

"I'd forgotten how many of you there are," he said. "Perhaps you have some shoes and boots for me to repair."

"Glad to hear you offer," said Father as he entered the room, carrying Baby Abigail. He handed the baby to Rebecca and sat down next to Enoch. "I will be returning to the front soon and I will need boots without worn soles. Do you think you can fix up some shoes for the baby here too?"

"No problem, sir," Enoch said. "The rest of you bring me your shoes and I will see if they need repair. That will help me repay your hospitality."

Enoch spent most of the day working. He made a cute pair of soft shoes for Baby Abigail and had just finished repairing all the other shoes we had piled in front of him when he turned to me and said, "Would you like to take a walk with me and stretch our legs?"

"Yes, sir, I mean Enoch. I would like to," I said. "I'll get my cloak."

We started out behind the house in the direction of the apple orchard. The fall breeze rustled the last dying leaves clinging to the sleeping branches. I didn't even think to bring a musket. His hand rested comfortably on my back as we walked, enjoying the fall air. I looked up at him. His nose still dominated his narrow face but his eyes sparkled as he talked. The deep lines around his nose and mouth had softened since his arrival. Happy lines radiated from his eyes accentuating his inviting demeanor. My heart flipped and flopped so I could hardly concentrate on what he was telling me. The birds seemed to sing louder and the wisps of hair that had fallen from my braid kept flying into my eyes. Enoch was telling me about his trip from Fishkill. He had run into the Skinners but had talked his way free by fixing one of the men's boots.

Suddenly he grew serious. He stopped and turned me around to face him. My heart beat so hard I thought he could surely hear it.

"Sybil, I need to ask you a question," he said. "Please answer me truthfully. You know I am a spy and that your father will be going back to the front soon. The committee will need to get me some messages while he is gone. Your father has offered your services as a courier for these messages."

"Yes," I answered, not daring to say more.

"Sometimes being a courier can be dangerous," he said. "Are you sure you want to do it?"

"I didn't have any problem the last time, did I?" I said in a voice that sounded too loud to my ears. "I can shoot as well as any militia soldier and I am just as clever as you are."

"You certainly fooled those guards at the prison," he said. "Our meeting place has been set. I will be at the Indian trail on the west side of White Pond every afternoon in case the committee needs to get me a message."

We turned without another word and walked back to the house. After supper the men on the committee arrived and the parlor doors remained closed. Father didn't even ask me to bring drinks to the men. I went up to bed, but couldn't fall asleep. I could hear the rumbling of deep voices well into the night. The voices sounded like rolling thunder in the distance punctuated by sharp outbursts. The risky business of war had reached into our cozy west parlor.

MILITIA PRACTICE
Chapter Thirteen
1776, 4 November

"Poise your firelocks!"

"Cock your firelocks!"

"Present!"

"Fire!"

I woke to a loud blast. I sat up, shook my head, and looked around. Mary and Rebecca were gone. A loud rumble of wagon wheels shook the floor. Why didn't anyone wake me? I rushed to the window and looked out. Below in the field were two hundred men lined up for battle. Around the perimeter were about twenty wagons filled with women and children watching and waiting for the drill to be over. I dressed quickly and rushed down stairs. Forgetting breakfast, I grabbed my cloak and ran out on the piazza. Mother was sitting and watching with Baby Abigail asleep in her arms.

"Why didn't you wake me?" I asked.

"You really have taken so much responsibility lately, I thought I'd let you sleep," Mother said. "You must have forgotten that today is the day your father set for mustering the troops for practice."

"All of the wives and children are here too," I said. "What will happen when they are done?"

"Each family brought food and baked goods," Mother said.

"When the men are done, we will all celebrate and eat together."

I sat for a while watching the drills. The young boys, too young to fight, kept the drill going with their fifes and drums. Each cadence signaled a different formation.

I was intrigued by the complexity of the drills. Smoke filled the air as the men fired their guns loaded only with paper wads. They didn't waste bullets on practice. I could only imagine what a real battle would be like. Father commanded the troops from his horse at the far end of the field.

"Sybil, go get Rebecca, and the two of you can stoke up the fire and start the water for tea," said Mother.

She knew the practice would end soon and we needed to provide for all our guests. I went down the front steps and out through the wagons looking for Rebecca. I finally found her talking and laughing with a few of the neighbor boys her age.

"Come on Rebecca. Mother wants us to start heating water for tea," I said.

"Can't I just stay here with my friends?" Rebecca asked. "You can get everything ready by yourself. You don't really need me, and I let you have some free time when Enoch visited. Now I need a turn."

"Fine, but next time it's my turn again," I said over my shoulder as I returned to the house.

I had just put the kettle of water on the fire to boil when Father came rushing into the kitchen.

"Sybil," he said. "Mother said you'd be in here. Come into the west parlor. I need to talk to you."

I didn't say a word, and followed him into the west parlor.

"Sybil, a rider just arrived from the committee. I must get a message to Enoch today. He is in danger if he doesn't leave Redding Corners tonight!"

"Will he meet me on the Indian trail on the west side of White Pond the way we planned?" I said.

"Yes," said Father. "You will have to disguise yourself as a boy. You can wear a pair of Archibald's breeches and one of my coats. Mother will pin your hair up under one of my hats. No one will recognize you. You must hurry because the journey is long. I want you home before dark. Ride Star and carry one of the muskets."

I rushed upstairs to get ready. Archibald's breeches were a snug fit but I managed to squeeze into them. Mother came up and fitted me in one of Father's old jackets that was too small for him. She helped me pin up my hair. I put on one of Father's hats and I was ready.

Father had saddled Star and met me behind the house carrying my musket.

"Look for rocks piled in sets of three," Father said. "Enoch and I set them out when we chose the spot."

"I'll find them, Father," I said.

I mounted, took the message and slid it safely into my boot, grabbed my musket and tucked it behind the saddle, and galloped off toward White Pond. My hands slipped on the reins and I wiped each one on my breeches. Was it fear or uncertainty that made my hands do this or was seeing Enoch again the cause? Would he really be at the meeting place?

I took a quick look behind me in case I was being followed but everyone was busy preparing the noonday meal. I could hear the fiddlers and flutes striking up as I rode off.

THE SHOEMAKER
Chapter Fourteen
1776, 4 November

I turned off at the Indian path and dismounted. Taking Star's reins, I led him deep into the woods. I discovered the first sign a few feet off the path and I soon picked out the next set hidden on the rocky hillside. After a while I came to a clearing and sat down to rest on a flat rock. This had to be the place. I was sure.

"Mr. Crosby," I whispered into the gloomy void, lit only by the light from the sun that danced its way to the ground forming small swatches on the pine-covered forest floor.

"Mr. Crosby, it's me," I said again.

"Yes, lad," answered a low voice just to my left. "What do you want?"

"It's me, Sybil," I said. "I bring word from Father. Don't you recognize me?"

With these words I whisked off my hat and my hair cascaded over my shoulders.

"Well, aren't you a sight," said Enoch as he stepped out of the shadows. "I didn't recognize you at all. What a pleasant surprise." He sat down next to me on the rock. I could smell the leather he carried to repair shoes and feel his warm breath close to my face.

"I bring you a message from the Committee on Safety," I said as

I reached down and withdrew the note from my boot. "They are waiting for your report that I am supposed to bring back. Also, my father said you're in danger if you don't leave tonight."

"Here is a list of a new group of Tory recruits. I will join them. I must return at once because they will rendezvous at Butter Hill in three days. You will be sure to get this message to your father?"

I took the report and looked at it.

"This is signed, John Smith. Why?" I asked.

"That's one of my aliases," he said. "You're sure the committee will get my report?" he asked again.

"You doubt that I can succeed," I said jumping up with a burst of courage and rage that I didn't know I had. I bent down and slipped the report deep into my boot. "Just because I am a girl, no one thinks I can do anything but cook, clean, and look after the children."

"Hold on a minute," said Enoch as he stood and put his hands on my shoulders. "You are a remarkable girl. You've taken extraordinary risks for me and you are helping the Patriot cause more than you know."

"I don't think so," I replied, looking down at my hands.

That's why I was so surprised at what happened next. Maybe I just wasn't ready. I don't know, but before I knew what had happened, Enoch's lips brushed against mine.

"I must be off," he said.

He turned and disappeared into the shadow of the tall trees. I stood stunned. My first kiss and I wasn't even ready. My heart raced and I could feel a warm glow creep up my face. Then suddenly a shiver rolled down my spine. Enoch's life was in danger. Would I see him again or would our first kiss be our last?

Star whinnied and poked my shoulder with his nose. I tucked my hair back up under the hat, took Star's reins, and led him back the way we had come.

THE SUMMONS
Chapter Fifteen
1776, 15 November

The first snow had fallen and the dark days of winter molded together like the grey bullets Father was wrapping with wadding. Each day rolled into the next. Father and the boys had finished stacking enough wood for the cold winter days ahead. The war seemed far away from our hearth until another messenger rode up to our front porch.

Father grabbed the musket and confronted the man at the door.

"Who goes there?" Father asked.

"A messenger from Captain Robinson at North Castle," the man shouted as he dismounted and clambered up the front steps. "Colonel Ludington, I bring you your orders from General Washington."

Father opened the door wider. The wind blew in, sending a chill over the east parlor. We all had been sitting by the hearth. Mother was spinning; Rebecca and I worked with our samplers, trying to teach Mary how to begin her letters. The boys played war with the wooden soldiers Father had carved for them. The wind blew the bullets Father had been wrapping onto the floor with a clatter.

The messenger lowered his voice and I concentrated to hear what was said.

"Colonel, you must return at once to North Castle because the fighting is intensifying," the messenger explained. "A few men have been killed and conspiracies are springing up like weeds in a hay field. Communications from the British in the south need to be intercepted and destroyed. The Skinners, who are ravaging our homes, must be caught and punished.

"I'll pack my gear and come," Father said. "Tell Major Robinson that my wife Abigail and the children will continue to host the meetings of the committee."

As suddenly as the messenger burst into our quiet afternoon, he left. The front door banged shut. With that, Father went upstairs to pack his gear. I put on my cloak and an old pair of Father's boots and ventured out in the snow to saddle up Father's horse. Rebecca and Mother went to the kitchen to ready some food for his journey.

No one said much and in the silence the sounds of the boys playing war resounded like those we had heard so often during the militia practice. The Thanksgiving feast and Christmas surprises would have to wait until Father returned home safely.

SKINNERS
Chapter Sixteen
1776, 29 November

Father had been gone for two weeks and the blowing snow covered the ground. Mother and I just finished the evening chores in the barn when we heard some horses gallop into the barnyard. We each grabbed a musket and I crept over to look out the partially open barn door. We had left it almost closed because of the strong wind.

I peered into the dusk and could see two strange men on horseback.

"I think they are Skinners," I whispered to Mother.

"We'll stand our ground," Mother whispered back.

I threw aside the barn door, and the wind caught it. A loud retort sounded as it slapped the side of the barn. I jumped. The light from our lanterns glowed out into the barnyard, silhouetting the two men against the cloudy sky.

"Stop, and state your business," I said, hoping I didn't sound as afraid as I was.

Mother and I readied our muskets on our hips. I could feel my heart pound and wondered if Mother felt the same.

"We've come to take your horses for the British cause," the first man stated in a flat voice. The men stayed where they were, waiting for our reaction.

One man dismounted and walked toward us.

"Stop where you are or I'll have to shoot," I said.

"What's a pretty girl like you doing with a musket?" the man asked, taking a few more steps toward us.

With that I lifted my musket to my shoulder and shot at his hat. The hat sailed back and landed in a snow drift. Mother raised her musket, and I started to reload. I can reload as fast as any militia fighter. Mother and I could not rely on only one warning bullet. I reached behind me and grabbed a cartridge from my pouch. I placed the stock of the gun on the ground and rammed the cartridge into the barrel. More hoofbeats sounded in the distance. Were more Skinners coming? Would they take Star and Blacky? When I raised my gun ready to shoot, a group of men galloped into the yard.

In the light from the barn, I recognized Mr. Jay and two other members of the Committee on Safety. I let out a huge breath that sounded like a sigh. The Skinner, who was standing, turned and jumped back on his horse and the two of them rode off toward the east woods. The two men with Mr. Jay continued on after them, but Mr. Jay stopped short and bounded to the ground.

"Are you all right, Abigail, Sybil?"

"Sybil shot the man's hat off and I was about to aim for his heart if necessary," Mother said.

"I'm sure I could have shot them," I said. I hoped Mr. Jay wouldn't notice my hands shaking. "I couldn't let them have Star and Blacky."

Mr. Jay walked over to the snowbank and picked up the hat. He twirled it on his finger.

"Look here," he said. "Your shot went clear through. Guess you showed him not to bother a lady, and a crack shot at that."

I blushed. A lady, he said, and a crack shot. Maybe Mother and I could have handled those Skinners alone, but I was sure glad Mr. Jay was early for his meeting tonight.

CHRISTMAS JOY
Chapter Seventeen
1776, 25 December

"Look, my winding top zooms across the floor," said Archibald.

"Watch mine go too," said Derick and Henry at the same time. The boys started winding the tops and sending them barreling across the floor of the west parlor.

We had just finished the huge Christmas dinner Mother had prepared. On the table were basins of carrots, potatoes, and turnips, a platter of wild turkey that Archibald had shot and dressed, fresh baked bread, and johnnycakes, with a dessert of pumpkin and apple pie. We girls were dressed in the new dresses Mother had made us from the fabric Rebecca and I brought back from Fishkill last fall. Baby Abigail wore her new tunic that Mother had made. She was experimenting with standing by pulling herself up using anything handy. We had a roaring fire in the fireplace and the room smelled of pine from the decorations. Our Christmas was pleasant but without Father, and his laughing and teasing, it wasn't the same.

Then we heard footsteps on the porch. I went to the window to see who was there while Mother rose and picked up the musket that leaned in the corner of the room. Outside, bracing himself against the howling wind and blowing snow, was Mr. Jay. I ran to the door to let him in.

"Jolly good spirits to all of you," said Mr. Jay as he brushed the snow off his coat. "I bring a special gift for the children and news of Henry."

"Has Father been wounded?" I asked before Mother could say a word.

"No, nothing like that," replied Mr. Jay. "Your father wanted to me to come and tell you he would be home before the first week in January."

Archibald, Henry, and Derick jumped up and started to do a little dance in a circle.

"Father's coming home," they chanted

"Here children, see what I brought you," Mr. Jay said over the joyous bunch.

He held out a book to me and I took it from him and curtsied.

"Thank you, sir," I said. I looked down at the title of the book, *Gulliver's Travels* by Jonathan Swift.

"I thought you children should have something new for your lessons," Mr. Jay explained turning to Mother. "Abigail, I must be on my way because the storm is getting worse. My family is expecting me to be home before too long, but I wanted to be sure you had the good news for Christmas. I will see you again, when we come for the meeting of the committee on January 8th."

With that, he turned and let himself out, latching the door behind him against the wind.

"Let me see the new book," said Mother with a smile in her eyes. I knew she had been keeping a brave face for the children, but now I could see she was truly happy. "I'll read the first chapter aloud before you go to bed tonight," she said.

What a wonderful surprise! We all were at peace knowing Father would be home soon. I went to the window and gazed out at the spitting snow. Where was Enoch on this cold wintry night? Was he captured again or was he spending Christmas with a family in the area?

SNOWBOUND
Chapter Eighteen
1777, 7 January

We all sat around the kitchen table to do our lessons. I had decided to give the children a treat and read another chapter of the book Mr. Jay gave us at Christmas. I had barely started to read, when Father rushed in. He had been home about a week and Rebecca and I were happy to have some relief from the chores and carrying water and wood.

"Sybil," he said in a breathless voice, "Mr. Crosby should be here by now."

He started to pace back and forth.

"I want you to ride out with me and look for him. He is carrying important information for the meeting of the committee tomorrow night."

My heart leapt into my throat. Enoch was coming here? If Father was worried, something must have happened. Maybe Enoch was shot or captured by Skinners.

"Go put your brother's breeches under your skirt to stay warm and get ready to go. You will ride Star and come with me in case I need help. Hurry, now," Father said, interrupting my thoughts.

I handed the book to Rebecca and ran upstairs to get the breeches and another warm shawl to put around my shoulders. The snow had already covered the front step when I stepped out on the porch. A northeast storm was brewing. While I was getting ready, Father had saddled the horses and was waiting for me at the front gate. Mother handed me some food, wrapped in cloth and a tin of water. I scurried down the steps to join him.

We started out toward White Pond. Star and I followed Father. The going was slow and the wind whipped my face. Small specks of ice stung my eyes. I leaned low on Star's mane to glean any heat the horse gave off. Father turned every so often to see if I was still following. My heart raced as I concentrated to keep Father in sight. After we had traveled for about an hour, Father stopped and waited for me to pull Star up beside him.

"We need to keep a lookout from here on out," he said.

"What are we looking for?" I asked.

"If Enoch was in trouble he would head for the meeting place at White Pond, but with this storm we might miss the turnoff because the snow has covered the trail markers," Father said as he brushed the snow out of his face.

He turned and urged his horse forward again. I followed.

We had gone about another half hour when I thought I spotted something. Tied to a sapling was a string of leather. If I hadn't been looking, I would have missed it.

"Father!" I yelled as I urged Star into a soft lope. "I see something."

Even against the wind, Father must have heard me because he pulled up on the reins and turned around.

"Over there. See that strip of leather tied to that sapling. That must be a signal from Enoch."

I turned Star into what I hoped was the Indian path that went to the usual meeting place near White Pond. Father followed. As we entered the woods, the darkness surrounded us like a cloak. The trees blocked the wind and suddenly the world became silent.

"Look, there's another strip of leather on that branch over there," I said. "Enoch must either be here or have traveled through."

Then I saw him. He was lying on the ground partially covered with snow. I could see his pack with his shoe repair supplies cast aside a few feet off. I urged Star forward and jumped to the ground when I reached Enoch. A chill ran through me and I shuddered. Was he dead? I couldn't see him breathing. Father came up behind me and we both leaned over the snow-covered man.

"Enoch, Enoch," said Father softly as he reached down and touched Enoch's shoulder. "Are you hurt?"

Enoch groaned and opened his eyes. His lips were blue and his face was red. I had never seen a person look like this before.

"Hello, sir," said Enoch. "I've got myself into quite a pickle I'm afraid. I've twisted my ankle on a rock and I have been lying here for quite a while."

Father lifted Enoch into a sitting position while I grabbed the food and water we had brought and offered them to him.

"You two are a sight for sore eyes," said Enoch. Even under these conditions his eyes sparkled when he looked up at me. I smiled back.

"Drink some of this water and have a bite of bread. That will help you get some of your strength back," said Father. "As soon as you are able, you will ride with us back to the house. We need to get you warmed up and ready to report to the committee at the meeting tomorrow."

I handed Enoch the water and our hands touched. My heart started to pound. Would both men be able to tell how I felt?

"You better ride Star, Enoch, and Sybil will mount with me. Can I help you mount? How bad is that ankle?" Father asked Enoch.

"I can't walk on it," Enoch replied. "Trust me, I've tried."

Father and I helped Enoch to stand on his good leg and we guided him toward Star. Star seemed to understand what was going on and stood stock still while Father helped lift Enoch up into the saddle. I ran to get his supplies, picked them up, and brushed off the snow. In spite of the cold, I could still smell the aroma of new leather. I handed the pack up to Enoch. Father waited for me to mount behind him and off we went toward home. We couldn't talk after we left the forest because the wind whipped the snow into our faces and roared in our ears. Three hours later we spotted the candles Mother had placed in the windows to help us find our way home in the storm.

MONOTONY
Chapter Nineteen
1777, 8 January

When we finally arrived home, Father and I hustled Enoch into the warm parlor. Mother removed his boots and tended to his ankle that soon swelled to double its size once his boot was off. Enoch seemed to revive with his usual high-spirited energy. I went to the kitchen to prepare supper for the three of us. The family had eaten earlier and the younger children were already in bed, so Father, Enoch and I sat down to a pleasant meal.

"You two are like my guardians. Every time I have a situation, you come to the rescue," said Enoch as he reached for his third serving of meat.

"I am glad I can help." I said.

"I have seen very little real fighting, myself. I spend most of my time traveling about looking for traitors," said Enoch.

As we ate Enoch entertained Father and me with stories of his adventures. I no longer felt like a child, but more like a grown woman. Would I be able to be alone with Enoch again?

The next night, on January 8th, the Committee on Safety met behind closed doors. I wasn't asked to bring in the drinks and cake. Father did it himself this time. The east parlor where I sat working on my sampler was silent except for an occasional outburst that came from the meeting in the west parlor. The children were in bed and Mother, Rebecca, and I sat and worked silently. We had nothing to say.

Three days after the meeting Enoch left. I hadn't been able to be alone with him at all between the children clamoring for his stories and Mother tending his ankle. I remembered his fleeting kiss. Did it really happen? That day seemed so long ago and I wondered if he thought of me as a woman, or only as Colonel Ludington's daughter.

I filled the nasty winter days with routine. There were lessons, meals to prepare, and chores to do. Messengers rode in and out bringing news of the battles and traitors, but Father kept the information to himself. If Mother knew what was happening, she kept silent too. No one mentioned Enoch, but he was all I could think about. One day melded into the next and at last the weather had started to break.

NORTHWARD BOUND
Chapter Twenty
1777, 3 February

"Sybil, come into the west parlor," Father said. "I need you to deliver a message to Enoch. He must head north to Albany County."

My heart jumped into my throat. Enoch was in danger if Father and the committee had ordered him to leave. He'll be gone and I'll never see him again.

"Where will I find him?" I asked, trying not to show my disappointment.

"Go to Fishkill and wait behind the church. You know the place. He was kept prisoner there last fall. Take the wagon. The journey will take you all day. If anyone stops you, pretend you're going to collect the French lace that your mother ordered. I can't go without arousing the suspicion of any Tories or Skinners who are lurking about the town, but an innocent girl will be ignored," replied Father.

Ignored? I should be used to that. How many times had I helped Father with his missions, yet he still sees me as a girl and a child. At least I'd get to see Enoch again before he went away for good.

"Hurry, Sybil, and get ready," Father said, breaking into my thoughts.

I put on some warm clothes and went to the kitchen to pack food for the trip. Mother must have known I would be going because a basket filled with bread, cheese, dried venison, and some apple cake sat on the kitchen table.

"Make sure you're careful," Mother said. "And don't forget to fetch the lace. I ordered it to make some new curtains for the parlor windows. Now go to your father and he will give you Enoch's orders."

I stared at her, surprised. Mother had always seemed oblivious of the events of war and yet here she was giving me orders. I returned to the west parlor where Father folded an official looking document, sealed it with his wax seal, and handed it to me. I tucked the letter into the small pocket in the hem of my skirt.

"Are you sure Enoch will be there?" I asked.

"He goes every fortnight to check for orders from the committee or Mr. Jay. He will meet you behind the church under the big oak tree where he has set up a temporary shop to fix shoes," said Father. "Hurry along now."

I took the basket and the musket, and then headed for the wagon. After stowing my supplies, I started out. I traveled all morning arriving in Fishkill in time to go to the fabric shop before it closed for lunch. I picked up the lace, stowed it in the wagon, and returned to the church. Tying the horse to the hitch in front of the church, I climbed down to look for Enoch. I spotted him chatting with some gentlemen who seemed to be looking at his wares. I could see him smiling and laughing as he entertained his customers. This time my mission was more complicated. Not wanting to arouse suspicion, I fetched the basket and walked over to the step of the church to sit down. The sun was shining, the winter air was crisp, and the wind was still. The stone step had been warmed by the sun. If I sat here, Enoch could see me and when the time was right perhaps he would walk over to talk. I removed my hat and let my hair fall to my shoulders remembering the time he hadn't recognized me before. I didn't want that to happen this time.

I took some meat and cheese from the basket, slid it between two pieces of Mother's fresh bread, and placed it back into the basket for Enoch. Then I put together a sandwich for myself. I took a big bite. The taste of Mother's bread reminded me of our warm kitchen at home as a sudden cold breeze sent chills down my spine. I looked over at Enoch. He was just as dashing as I remembered and I couldn't keep my eyes off him. Suddenly he looked up and his eyes met mine. I cast my eyes down, and then I looked toward him and grinned. He couldn't intimidate me. At least that's what I hoped my expression said. He said something to the men gathered around him, packed up his supplies, and jogged over to me.

"Well, if it isn't my favorite angel," he said laughing. "And what do you have here?"

"A lovely picnic on a cold winter's day," I retorted. "Would you care to join me?"

"Let's move to the cemetery side of the church so we won't be noticed. There is a big rock where we can sit. Enoch picked up the basket and guided me around the side of the church. There we sat down on the rock. I handed him his sandwich. He took an enormous bite and I watched as his eyes lit up.

"Your bread sure melts in my mouth," he said as he gobbled down another bite.

I laughed to myself. Every time I met the man I was feeding him or rescuing him.

"Would you like some cider to go with your lunch?" I asked. I pulled out two tin cups and began to pour from a small carafe I had propped in the basket. My hand shook as I poured a cup for both of us. Neither of us spoke as we sipped the cool cider.

I hoped anyone who happened along would think we looked like a young couple stealing a little time for a picnic lunch.

"Did you bring me something besides this lovely feast?" asked Enoch.

With that question, I reached down and retrieved Father's letter from its hiding place in my secret pocket, and concealed it in my palm. My heart raced when I lay my hand on Enoch's, and our fingers touched.

"Bend close to me," Enoch said.

He took the letter and broke the seal. As he read the order, his eyes clouded over and he scowled.

"Is something wrong?" I asked.

"The committee is sending me north to search for traitors in Albany. They are afraid my identity has been discovered. I must leave as soon as possible. My mission may be compromised if someone figures out what I'm up to," he said.

My lips trembled. I said nothing, afraid of betraying my feelings for him.

"I haven't been able to see you since you rescued me from the storm," he said.

"And now you are going away and I may never see you again."

The chilling wind blew and the icy air washed over my shoulders. I shivered.

Enoch slid his arm around my shoulders and drew me close. My heart raced. I felt the warmth of his body through his wool jacket.

He pressed his lips against my hair for a few seconds, and then got to his feet.

"I'd better be off," he said. "Be careful going back. He cupped my chin in his hand. I won't forget about you. When this war is over we may meet again."

"Be safe, Enoch," I said, feeling my throat tighten. I couldn't say any more or I knew I would cry. His duty called, and there was nothing I could or should do.

He picked up his pack, walked away toward the road, then turned once and waved before he disappeared from view.

I sat there on the rock, stunned. I would never be a child again. The turbulence of war had enveloped my heart.

I stood up, packed my basket, and returned to the wagon. No one even gave me a second look as I slapped the horse with the reins and headed toward home. The clouds covered the sun and the winter wind stung my face. I could feel my tears freeze as I tried to blink them away.

RIDE WITH FATHER
Chapter Twenty-one
1777, 11 March

We had just finished eating our noonday meal and Father asked me to get him a second piece of apple cake.

"I never get to do anything exciting since you and that committee sent Enoch away," I said as I cut a slice of cake and dumped it on his plate so hard that it toppled over onto the top.

"What's the matter with you, Sybil?" Father asked. "I would think you would be happy to stay at home and help your mother with the children. I've put you through enough danger already."

"I am a girl, and you don't think I'm as brave as a son would be but it's not true."

"Sybil, you know how much I think of what you have done for the war effort, Father argued. "I can't ask you to do any more."

"You aren't asking me. I feel so helpless. I can keep a secret and I can ride and shoot with the best boys my age. You go out often to check on the militia men. Why can't I ever go with you? Isn't there some way I can help?"

"It's not safe for a young girl to be riding off."

"But you'll leave me here alone with Mother to take care of things while you are at the front."

"Well then, I plan to spend the rest of the day and partway into the night riding out to check on the men in my regiment again. Perhaps you'd be willing to accompany me," Father said.

I forgot to be mad. I ran to Father and gave him a big hug.

"Thank you, Father," I said.

"Go change into a pair of my old breeches, grab one of my jackets, and pack up something for us to eat," said Father. "I'll saddle up the horses."

Fifteen minutes later we were off in the direction of Shaw's Pond. I hadn't traveled this way very often and I was amazed at how well Father knew the territory. As we rode by houses tucked into the hillsides, Father told me about the families who lived there. Shaw's Pond came up suddenly after we had ridden about two hours. Father stopped in front of a house, dismounted, and handed me his reins.

"This is the house of one of my men," Father explained. "I'll just be a short while. I want to know how he and his family are and if he is ready if we need to muster the troops."

I waited patiently and soon Father was back. He mounted with a flourish and we were off again.

"We'll head on to Mahopac, talk to a few men there, and then we'll go as far as Mahopac Falls," he said. "We can't stay too long because the trip back will be slower since it will be nightfall."

Time passed quickly as we visited the last few houses. Turning around, we headed toward home. All I could think of was how Father trusted me. The road was deserted at this late hour so Father and I rode side by side.

Suddenly a shot rang out as it hit a tree off to my right. Star jumped and took off at a gallop. I crouched low on his neck not knowing who had shot at us or why. I could hear Father's horse,

Blacky, behind me. Was it some Skinners trying to steal our horses or was it someone trying to collect the ransom that was still on Father's head? We continued at full speed until Father pulled up beside me and signaled me to rein up. He reached over and put his hand on my arm and pointed. Then I understood what he wanted. Ahead, at the edge of the woods off to the right, I saw the three stones that marked the entrance to the hidden Indian path where I had met Enoch to deliver him the messages. I felt a twinge in my heart as I thought of him now. Was he being held in some dark prison or was he sitting at some stranger's dining room table entertaining another young girl with his stories? I turned into the path and Father followed. The bushes closed around us just in time.

"Here they come," said Father in a whisper. "Those are bound to be Skinners who wouldn't think twice about stealing our horses and leaving us to walk the rest of the way home."

We dismounted and waited. I could hear the sound of the horses' hooves as they pounded past our hiding place. Would they find us? Luck was with us. The night stayed silent.

"We'll cross the road quickly because there is a path through the woods that'll take us home," Father said. "We can't take any chances on the main road because the Skinners might come back looking for us. Follow me."

I nodded and followed him into the woods on the other side.

Father seemed to know every tree and path. Night had come and I could hear the small animals scurry away as we passed. The horses seemed to understand that something was amiss as they stepped on the soft forest floor without making a sound. We continued like that for about another half hour without a word. I looked up at the sky and only the light from the moon and the stars filtered through the trees.

"How can you tell which way to go?" I asked at last.

"I just leave the North Star ahead and a little to the left," said Father. "We don't have to travel too much further."

We came out into a clearing and I recognized our apple orchard. What a surprise! I had explored the woods on almost every side of our farm but I never knew I could get home this way. In the attic window, Mother had put a lantern.

Father galloped ahead of me through the orchard and into the barnyard. We fed and brushed down the horses and headed for the house.

"Where have you been?" Mother asked when we stepped into the kitchen. "You were supposed to be back before dark Henry, especially when you have Sybil with you."

"It was slow going thanks to the Skinners who chased us so we had to come home through the orchard. I was glad to see you put the lantern out for us," Father said with a chuckle.

Mother gave us each some hot sassafras tea before sending me off to bed. As I tried to fall asleep, I could hear them talking in the kitchen below. Father must discuss the war with Mother more than I realized.

CIDER AND CAKE
Chapter Twenty-two
1777, 5 April

"Turning sixteen doesn't really make any difference to me," I said to Father as I gobbled up my last bite of apple cake. "If I were a boy, I would enlist tomorrow and fight for the Patriots."

"Your birthday is important to us," said Mother. "You are a courageous girl and have done more than most to fight the British."

"Now that Enoch's gone, the Committee on Safety has no more use for a girl except to serve them cake and cider when they have their meetings."

We sat around the table celebrating my sixteenth birthday. Mother had made me a new dress with more ruffles and a lower neckline. I loved the dress but there was no one to wear it for. Enoch had gone north to Albany and I would probably never see him again. My birthday seemed only to mark the monotonous passing of time.

"Sybil, Sybil," said Archibald as he jumped up from the table. "Play Fox and Geese with me, please," he pleaded.

I could always count on Archibald to snap me out of my doldrums.

"Sure," I said. "Go get the beans and the board and set up the game. The rest of you can watch and Rebecca will play the winner."

Archibald put the geese, which were the white beans, on each cross of the lines and I set the black bean in the middle. We played with lots of excitement until Archibald had my fox cornered and blocked in. He won the game and Rebecca took over for her turn.

Rain began to pound on the roof and the wind blew in gusts that caused the branches of the bushes around the house to scrape the windows like animal claws on the bark of a tree. Winter was departing with a fury that echoed the war being waged far away.

I stood up and went to get my cloak.

"Shall I go out and check the horses in the barn?" I asked.

"I'll go with you," Father replied.

We wrapped ourselves in our wool cloaks and slipped out the back door trying not to let the cold wet air invade the warm kitchen. Out of habit, I grabbed the musket and tied the pouch of bullets at my waist. The wind licked our cloaks like a hungry animal.

The sleet-filled rain stung our faces. We bent our heads against it and trudged toward the barn without speaking. I looked up and saw two horses tied to the tree on the north side of the barn. Father signaled me to be ready and drew his pistol from under his cloak. My heart thundered in my chest. The wind whipped the barn door back against the wall of the barn with a loud crack when Father opened it. Two men jumped up and pushed past us to make their escape. As one of the men lumbered past, I swung my musket with all my strength. I heard a loud crack as the musket hit the man across the neck and chin. The man yelped like a wounded animal and grabbed his neck with both hands.

"Get out of our barn, you nasty thieves!" Father shouted, aiming his pistol at the second man.

"Sorry sir," the taller man whined as he held up his hands. "We didn't know this was your farm. We're not Skinners. We are enlisted men making our way to Fishkill to join our regiment. Please don't shoot."

"What is the regiment password for traveling through this way if you don't want me to tie you up and take you to Fishkill as a prisoner of war?" said Father.

The taller man mumbled something I couldn't hear because the wind caught the barn door and it slammed shut again with another loud crack. It must have been correct though, because Father led them back into the barn.

"Sybil, go to the house and find something for these weary men to eat while I help them bed down their horses," Father said.

I ventured out into the storm and made my way back to the house. Mother and I prepared a basket of bread, warm beef stew, and a few slices of my birthday cake. When I returned to the barn, I could see the bruise on the man's face and neck where I had hit him. He smiled at me anyway.

"Great way for me to start out my enlistment duties," he said, laughing. "I never thought I'd be beaten by a girl, and a pretty one at that."

I blushed and said nothing. Spreading a cloth on a bag of feed, I set out the food Mother and I had fixed.

"What's the cake for?" one of the men asked.

"My birthday," I said with a smile.

"Happy birthday," the two men said in chorus.

I felt guilty as I watched the bruise get bigger and bigger on the man's neck, but they could have been the enemy.

War certainly brought out the best and worst in people.

MESSAGE FROM DANBURY
Chapter Twenty-three
1777, 26 April

"Father," I shouted, "a strange man is approaching on horseback."

"Rebecca, you take the boys upstairs. Sybil, you get the musket and stand guard behind the door. I will accost this stranger to find out what business he has with us at this late hour."

We had all been sitting in the east parlor enjoying the warmth of the fire on a cold rainy evening. The rain raged at the window where I had been keeping watch with one eye and doing my sewing with the other. The boys had been playing Fox and Geese and Mother was still upstairs putting Tertullus and Baby Abigail to bed. I jumped up from my post, grabbed the musket from its usual spot, and scurried behind the door. I could hear the pounding of the man's boots on the steps as Father opened the front door. The rain pelted the floor in front of Father's feet through the open door.

"Who goes there?" Father demanded.

"A messenger from Danbury," shouted a bedraggled man as he stumbled through the door. "I bring grave news. The British are burning the town and our supplies are gone. General Tryon and two thousand British troops are ravaging the town. Nothing is left. You can see the glow of the raging fire, there in the eastern sky. Orders are to muster the 7th Regiment and join Generals Arnold and

Wooster to repel the British and send them back to the sea."

Father helped the messenger to the nearest chair and stepped outside to look up at the eastern sky. I followed. The glow of destruction lit up the stormy sky, and the rain pelted down like the tears of a mourning widow.

"Sybil, go get your mother. The messenger must ride to muster the troops to march," said Father.

I ran down the hall, stowed the musket in its familiar corner, and took the stairs two at a time.

"Mother, come quickly, Father needs you to help with the messenger. He is tired and wet and must continue on his journey to muster the troops. The British have burned Danbury and are headed this way. We must stop them," I said.

Mother came out of the children's bedroom and closed the door softly.

"Hush," she said. "You'll wake the baby. What did you say about Danbury?"

I repeated the message as the two of us went downstairs. Mother took one look at the messenger then stared at Father in disbelief.

"This man can't ride any more," she said to Father. "He's exhausted. Also he doesn't know the route. You will have to muster the troops yourself."

"That's not possible and there are no neighbors near enough to call. Archibald is too young. I must be here to rally the troops and there is no one to send," said Father.

"I can go," I said. "I know most of the route from our rides in March. I'm sixteen and if I were a boy, I would be fighting already. Let me go, Father, please?"

"She can't go," said Mother. "I need her here and the trip is too dangerous. Look at the messenger and see what the twenty-three miles in this weather has done to him."

"I know I can do it. I'm sure I can," I said again.

"There is no one else," said Father. He turned to me. "Go upstairs and dress in my breeches. Be sure to put on two of my shirts and grab your cloak. I will saddle Star and Mother will pack a small bit of bread and cheese for the journey."

I went back upstairs and dressed in the clothes Father had suggested. I pinned my hair on top of my head and tied a scarf tightly around my neck for warmth. As I came downstairs, Mother handed me my cloak and wrapped it tightly around me. She handed me a pack containing the food wrapped in an old wool rag then hugged me tight. I watched as her eyes filled with tears.

"I'll be fine," I said leaning over to kiss her cheek. "Don't worry, I'll be home by morning."

I grabbed the musket and headed out the front door. Outside, Father stood with Star, ready to go. The horse must have sensed our urgency because he pawed the wet ground with his front hoof.

"Good luck, Sybil," Father said as he tied the musket to the back of the saddle. "You're a brave girl and a faithful daughter. Take this stick to prod Star when the going gets rough and to bang on the shutters at the houses of my militia leaders. You remember them all from our trip in March, right?"

"Yes I do, Father. I'll be careful and I'll stop at Hasbrouck's before I head home," I said bending down and kissing his cheek.

I nudged Star into a trot and started down the road. Why were there tears mingling with the rain on my cheeks, I wondered?

MUSTERING THE TROOPS
Chapter Twenty-four
1777, 27 April

I brushed the tears from my face. This was no time for tears. That messenger had only ridden from Danbury and the distance I must cover was a lot further than that. I leaned down and patted Star on the neck as I nudged him to go faster. We started off into the rain in the direction of Shaw's Pond.

"We can do it," I told him.

The rain fell in sheets all around us and the night was black. Star knew the road and he galloped fast, his hoofs splashing mud up on my breeches as we traveled along. I looked up at the trees and tried to see the edge of the road by looking at the darker shadows against the cloudy night sky. The rain stung my face and eyes, but every few minutes lightning flashed and lit my way.

A lightning-bolt zigzagged its way to the ground ahead, followed by a loud crack and then a thump. Star came to an abrupt stop, sliding on the muddy road. I grabbed his mane to keep myself from sliding over his head. I steadied myself.

"What's the matter, boy?" I asked, patting his neck to reassure him.

The sky lit up with more lightning and then I could see. A huge tree had fallen, blocking the road. I slid off the horse, grabbed the reins, and looked for a way around. I shivered. If I had ridden any faster, both Star and I would have been crushed by the weight of the tree. My heart raced and my boots sunk into the deep mud.

As soon as I rounded the tree I mounted again and rode off, arriving at Shaw's Pond a while later. There were only a few lights in the windows of the sleeping houses. At the first militia leader's house, I took the stick Father had given me and banged it against the closed shutters.

"Hurry, Danbury is burning!" I yelled above the wind and rain. "Look to the east and see the red sky. The British are burning Danbury. Muster at Ludington's at dawn."

The window opened and a man stuck his head out. I recognized him from my rides in March.

"Ride on, Sybil," he shouted waving me on. "I will alert the rest of the men here. Ride on and Godspeed to Mahopac."

I waved and turned Star back to the road that led down to Mahopac. The rain had turned the road into mud and the going was as slippery as an ice storm in winter. My soaked cloak hung on my arms like stone and I began to feel a chill. My fingers and toes were numb and Star slowed. His feet kept slipping out from under him. I thought we would never reach our destination. Then I saw the lake on the right and the town with only a few lights showing on this nasty night. I rapped at the first house and the second and on through the town.

"Danbury is burning! Muster at Ludington's at dawn!" I shouted at each house. I rode around Mahopac Pond and on toward Red Mills where I knew I could take a short rest and eat some of the food I was carrying. I had to slow Star to a walk because the road was like a river. We plodded along and the thunder and lightning continued to punctuate the darkness. My ears roared with the constant howling of the wind.

"You're the best horse ever!" I cried to Star as he slipped on the ascent to Kent's Cliffs. "Keep it up, boy! We'll make it!"

My words seemed to spur him on and soon I could see the light Mrs. Hasbrouck always kept burning to show the way for weary travelers. I banged on the shutter and shouted my message. After a moment, the front door of the inn swung open and I could see Mrs. Hasbrouck motioning me to dismount and come in. Gladly, I accepted her invitation.

"My husband will bring some water for your horse, Sybil, while you take a short rest and have a bit of warm cider," she said. "We'll hang your cloak by the fire so it will dry a bit while you rest."

I sat down and gobbled up the soggy food Mother had given me and sipped some of Mrs. Hasbrouck's hot cider. The liquid warmed my insides as it trickled down my throat.

"I'm so grateful for your hospitality," I told Mrs. Hasbrouck as I swallowed the last drop of cider, "but I must continue on to Stormville. I have a long way to go and many men to muster."

I put on my soggy cloak, thanked her again, and went back out into the storm.

Star seemed rejuvenated after his short rest and long drink. Up the hill we climbed to Stormville and shouting my message, I banged again on the shutters of the Patriots.

"Muster at Ludington's at dawn! The British are burning Danbury! Look to the red glow in the east!" I cried.

The bell at the church started to ring, calling the men in the countryside. Satisfied, I started back home toward Pecksville. Now the rain had abated and the wind was still. Star and I rode in silence and all I could hear was the slurping sound of his hooves as he trotted along the muddy road. We didn't have far to go now, I thought. That's when I spotted a campfire glowing in the woods on the left side of the road.

I pulled up on Star's reins and dismounted. The campfire belonged to a band of Skinners, I was sure. They were the only ones who would be out on a night like this. I wasn't going to take any chances that they would catch me and steal Star. I took the reins and led him off the road on the other side and into the woods. Keeping my hand on his nose so he would stay quiet, we continued on through the woods until I was sure we'd traveled well beyond the Skinners campfire. Coming back on the road, I looked around.

The rain had lifted and the clouds no longer covered the whole sky. I spotted the North Star that Father had shown me, and felt a familiar warmth flow through me. I mounted and Star trotted off leaving the North Star ahead and little to the left. Arriving at Pecksville, I banged again on the shutters of each house, shouting my message for all to hear. Men gathered in the square.

"Muster at Ludington's!" I shouted, and then off I rode toward home.

Night had lifted and the sun rose, adding its glow to the already red eastern sky as I rode toward home. Fog from the heavy rain covered the countryside. In the morning mist I saw men pass me on horseback carrying their muskets by their sides. Other militiamen walked along the side of the road. They waved at me and I waved back. As I rode into our yard, I could see Father drilling his men. Hundreds of them had already mustered. The men had come from all over, willing to fight for the cause of freedom and independence.

"Sybil, you're safe!" yelled Mother when she saw me. She ran down the steps of the front porch and grabbed Star's reins. "I knew you must be safe when the men started to arrive. Take Star to the barn and go get some rest."

I took Star's reins and led him to the barn. Father saw us and waved. Seeing him wave, the men broke rank and turned to wave with him. I waved back satisfied that I had made a difference. I wondered if the men would be in time to save Danbury or whether their houses would be burned and their families murdered. Star's whinny broke into my thoughts as I reached his stall. He seemed to say that he knew he'd done his job well. I brushed him down, gave him some water and hay, and dragged myself to the house.

THE BATTLE OF RIDGEFIELD
Chapter Twenty-five
1777, 3 May

A week later a messenger arrived about noon while I was sitting on the porch giving the children their lessons. He sprung from his horse, tied the reins around the hitch, and bounded up the front steps. I recognized him as one of the Kent cousins, and rose to meet him. For once I didn't need to reach for the musket and hide the children from view.

"Good morning," said the messenger, bowing in front of me. "You must be Sybil. You are prettier than the stories about you made me believe."

I blushed but held his gaze. I had no intention of being intimidated by the likes of this bedraggled messenger-boy, from the neighborhood or not.

"May I speak to your mother, please?" he asked.

"Surely you can give me any message you have for Mother," I replied, holding out my hand.

"This is a report from Colonel Ludington and I was ordered to deliver it to his wife," he said.

"Very well then, I'll fetch her."

I walked slowly into the kitchen, took Baby Abigail from Mother and told her about the messenger.

After lunch, while the children were napping, Mother called Archibald, Henry, Derick, Mary, Rebecca, and me into the east parlor.

"Children, here is a letter from your father," she said. "He will return home in a few days, but he wanted me to read you this letter."

1777, 2 May   *Ridgefield*

My dear Abigail and loving children,

This letter comes from a proud father and loving hus-band. After Sybil's long and dangerous ride to muster the troops, our 7th militia started out for Danbury to help the other militia forces push back the British. Regrettably we learned from a messenger that we arrived too late and much of Danbury was lost. We changed our course and headed for Ridgefield. Here we began to erect a barricade. General Wooster, with two hundred of his men, began the battle by attacking the British rear guard and capturing several pris-oners. On his second charge, the British mortally wounded General Wooster and word of his death reached us this morning. His heroic effort gave us time to prepare our defensive position. When General Tryon reached our posi-tion, he advanced on us from all three fronts outnumbering us by more than three men to our one. We held our ground for a while, but were forced to withdraw under General Arnold's orders with twelve dead and many wounded. Sporadic fighting continued all day and the British finally controlled the town. They set up camp just south of Ridgefield and the next morning they retreated just in time. Six hours later they left for their ships at Compo Beach.

Thousands of our soldiers had been rallied to this area and our success was apparent. We hope that the British will desist from ever launching another inland battle in Connecticut.

Sybil, talk of your ride has spread through the troops and I am proud I have a daughter with such courage. Your help enabled our militia to aide in turning the tide of the British advance. General Washington sent a letter congratulating us and in it he stated he would come and thank you himself.

I remain your loving husband and father.

Henry

I smiled to myself. Would Enoch hear of my exploits? Would I ever see him again? I didn't know. But I would always remember my first kiss deep in the woods and the sparkle in his eyes that warmed my heart. What about General Washington's visit? Should I wear the new dress that I got for my birthday?

AFTERWORD

Seven years after her heroic ride, in 1784, Sybil married Edmound Ogden, a lawyer. In 1792 they moved to the village of Catskill. She had one child, Henry, and in 1799 her husband died. In 1803 she became an innkeeper. Later in 1811, Sybil, her son Henry, and her daughter-in-law moved to Unadilla. Her son had six children and just as she had helped raise her brothers and sisters, Sybil stayed with her son to help raise her grandchildren. Sybil died in 1839 and was buried next to her parents behind the church where she grew up.

It is not known if Sybil ever saw Enoch Crosby again but perhaps she read his letter in the "Journal of Commerce" thanking the citizens of New York where he attended a special performance of "The Spy" given in his honor.